Snow Tales

Snow Tales

Two Tales from the Frozen North

MICHAEL MORPURGO
Illustrated by Michael Foreman

DOUBLEDAY

SNOW TALES
A DOUBLEDAY BOOK 978 0 857 53188 9

THE RAINBOW BEAR
First published in Great Britain by Doubleday, an imprint of Random House Children's Books
A Random House Group Company

LITTLE ALBATROSS
First published in Great Britain by Doubleday, an imprint of Random House Children's Books
A Random House Group Company

This collection first published as
Snow Tales by Doubleday in 2012

1 3 5 7 9 10 8 6 4 2

The Random House Group Limited supports the Forest Stewardship Council® (FSC®), the leading
international forest certification organization. Our books carrying the FSC label are printed on
FSC®-certified paper. FSC is the only forest certification scheme endorsed by the leading
environmental organizations, including Greenpeace. Our paper procurement policy can be
found at www.randomhouse.co.uk/environment.

Set in Mrs Eaves

Random House Children's Books, 61–63 Uxbridge Road, London W5 5SA

www.kidsatrandomhouse.co.uk
www.totallyrandombooks.co.uk
www.randomhouse.co.uk

Addresses for companies within The Random House Group Limited
can be found at: www.randomhouse.co.uk/offices.htm

THE RANDOM HOUSE GROUP Limited Reg. No. 954009

A CIP catalogue record for this book is available from the British Library.

Printed in China

CONTENTS

For dear Ted, who taught me how bears shed
rainbows, and so much more besides.
M. M.

The Rainbow Bear

I am snow bear. I am sea bear. I am white bear. I wander far and wide, king in my wild white wilderness.

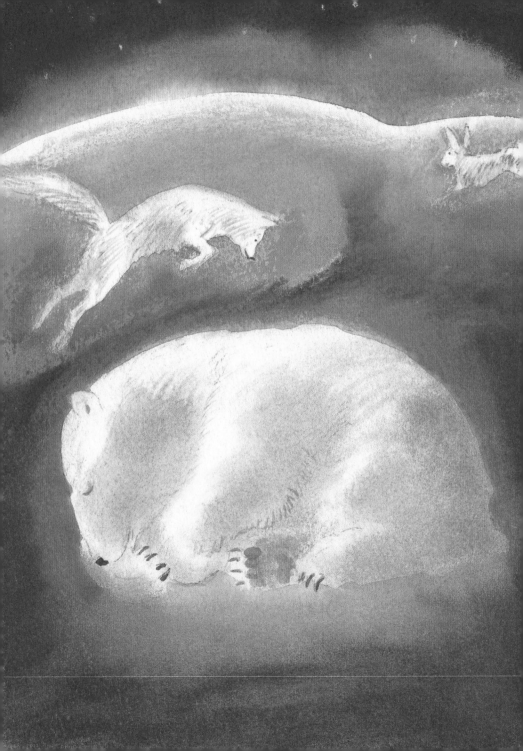

The snow has darkened around me
again. I have dug my den deep into
the mountainside. Here I am warm.
Here I shall dream away the winter . . .

There will be plenty of hopping hares
to pounce on. But hares are tricky.
Plenty of frisking foxes. But foxes
are fast. Plenty of wallowing
walruses. But walruses are big.

Seals are slow. Seals are best. I stalk them
silently. Silently. I am snow bear in a world
of white and they cannot see
me coming. But one sound,
and a seal slips away into the sea.

A seal in the sea is slippery quick. Narwhals
and beluga whales are strong, too strong.

Fish flash by like silver light and are gone before they were ever there. Here all about me is whooping and whistling of whales. Here is groaning and grinding of ice. Here I am snow bear no more. I am green and blue and indigo and turquoise. Here I am sea bear.

I clamber out of the sea. I shake myself dry in the sun. I am snow bear again. I look about me.

Rainbow! Rainbow over my wild white wilderness. Beautiful and bright he was, more wonderful than anything I had ever seen before.

I knew at once I had to catch rainbow
and make him mine. So I went after him.
I went hunting rainbow.

I leapt from ice floe to ice floe.
I galloped through snow. Ever closer,
ever closer. I stalked him silently.
Silently. And there at last was rainbow,
just one leap away. I pounced.

But I pounced on snow, on white
white snow. Rainbow was gone,
vanished with the wind. I lay in wait
for him, for days, for nights, but he
never came back. So I went looking
for him. I roamed my wild white
wilderness. I would hunt nothing
but rainbow.

How long I wandered I did not know.
I was weary. I was hungry. I knew
I must eat, or I would die.

I smelt man. Then I saw man. Man is
clever. Man is danger. But this man was
alone and I was hungry. This man was
sitting on the ice. He was fishing.

I stalked him silently. Silently.
When he saw me, he did not
try to run. There was no fear
in his eyes, only wisdom.

"So, my friend," he said, "so you
have come to eat me. I'm old,
very old, I'm not much of a meal
for a king of a bear like you."

And it was true. He was old,
little more than skin and bone.
But a meal was a meal. I made
ready to pounce.

"Only leave me to live out my days,
my friend," he went on, "and I
shall grant you your dearest wish.
For I am wiser than man."

"I am shaman. I know all there is to know.
I know you hunt rainbow. But rainbow
cannot be hunted, cannot be caught.
All you can do is let rainbow come to you.
And when he does, you must not pounce on
him, you must wish on him. Then all you
wish will come true. This I promise you."

The wise old shaman turned back to his
fishing again.

So I walked off and left him there on the ice.
I did just as he had told me. I hunted no more
for rainbow, only for seal and fox and hare.
But I still looked everywhere for rainbow.

Every night I dreamt of him. Then one
morning I woke and rainbow was there.
It was him!

It was rainbow
leaping out over
the sea and across
the sky towards me.
I remembered again the wise
old shaman's words. So I sat
on my mountainside and waited,
and hoped. And waited and hoped.

Nearer he came, nearer still, until he stopped right over me. I was soaked through in his colours. I was rainbow too! I knew at once what to wish for.

I closed my eyes and I wished. "Let me only stay like this, just as I am at this moment. Let me be rainbow bear."

When at last I opened my eyes, rainbow had gone from the sky above me. But I was rainbow, rainbow all over! I was rainbow bear!

I cavorted, I frolicked. I tumbled down the mountainside. I rolled in the snow. I plunged into the sea. When I came out I shook myself dry. I was still rainbow bear! No bear before me had ever been happier than I was then.

I went to find the old
shaman, to tell him,
to show him. It was far to
go, so I hunted as I went.
I smelt seal. I stalked him
silently. Silently. But seal
saw me coming and was
quickly gone. I smelt fox.
I stalked him silently.
Silently. But fox saw me
coming and was quickly
gone. I smelt hare. I stalked
him silently. Silently. But
hare too saw me coming
and was quickly gone.

By the time I found the wise
old shaman again, I was weak
with hunger.

"Ah, my friend," he said. "Wherever I
go they speak of little else but you.
Out at sea, the whales whistle and whoop
of it. The waves murmur it. At night
the snowy owl hoots to the moon of it.
And all say the same: 'Have you seen
the rainbow bear? Is he not the most
beautiful bear the world has ever seen?'
And you are. But there is much danger
in beauty, my friend."

And even as he spoke, he pointed out to
sea. A great ship was stealing towards us
through the ice floes, silently. Silently.
"Look!" he cried. "They have come for
you, my friend. Run! Hide yourself!
Go, before it is too late!"

So I ran and ran,
but the men from the
great ship came after me
with their dogs and their guns.

I hid where I could, but wherever I hid
they found me. I was no longer a white
bear in a white world. I made for my
mountainside, for my winter den. But
the men soon dug me out. I was too weak
to fight the net they threw over me.

"We have him!" they cried. "We have the rainbow bear! Let's take him back to the ship. He'll make us a fortune."

And so they took me away.

Oh, I had everything I had wished for. I was indeed rainbow bear, but my kingdom was now a cage. I could see the moon, I could see the stars — all through the bars of my cage.

In their thousands, they came to stare at me, to laugh at me. My only escape was in my dreams. But when I dreamt it was always of the wild white wilderness I had left behind and would never see again. I would be white bear again, white bear hunting, white bear stalking. But always I woke, and always the bars were still there.

And so my days passed, each day as long as a winter, each day the same — until early one morning when a voice roused me from my dreams.

"Mr Bear," came the voice. "Oh, Mr Rainbow Bear." A small boy was gazing up at me through the bars of my cage.

"I've been watching you, Mr Rainbow Bear," said the boy. "You just sit there and rock. You just walk up and down. You hate it in there. You hate being a rainbow bear, don't you? You're thinking, I want to be like other snow bears, I want to be back home where I belong, in all that ice and snow, with all those seals and walruses."

Suddenly he was up on the wall and pointing at the sky. "Look, Mr Rainbow Bear!" he cried. "Just like you! It's a rainbow, a rainbow!"

"Don't you know, don't you know? Just find the end of a rainbow and you'll have all the world to wish for. It's coming closer, closer. It's coming right over us now! We're at the very end of the rainbow. Quick! You wish. I'll wish. We'll both wish together."

He closed his eyes and lifted his hands into the rainbow above us. Now he was rainbow all over, just as I was.

"We wish this bear was white," cried the boy. "We wish this bear could go back home where he belongs, where he'll be happy. Now, this very minute."

And the boy wished, and I wished with him. I wished myself white. I wished myself away, and back home.

I am waking up, waking up. I have been dozing long enough down in my den. Time to get up. Time to hunt. There's the light of spring seeping through the snow above. I'll dig myself out.

Blue, blue sky. Eye-dazzling sun. Wonderful
sun. New air. Icy air. I breathe in deep.
The long winter sleep is done and forgotten
now. How I wish I could remember my
dreams. But I never can.

I clamber out. I cavort, I frolic, I tumble
down the mountainside. I roll in the snow.

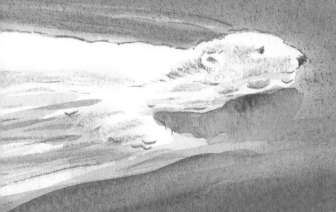

I plunge into the sea. It is so good to
be alive, so good to be wild.

I am snow bear. I am sea bear. I am white
bear. I wander far and wide, king in my
wild white wilderness.

For Ben and Clara.
M. M.

Little Albatross

The last snows of winter were melting
away. Still, so still sat Mother Albatross,
looking out over a grey-green sea.

Underneath her, snug in the warmth
of her feathers, Little Albatross slept.
He was only a few hours old, and
already strong with life.

Far out at sea Father Albatross soared above the waves, his great wide wings beating his way homewards. And he was full of the fish he had caught.

"Welcome home!" cried Mother Albatross, proud as a mother always is.

Still in his dreams Little Albatross smelt fish for the first time.

"Feed me, Father," he begged. "Feed me."

"That's what we're here for," said Father Albatross.

Little Albatross ate all he could, and then slept again.

After that, Mother and Father took it in
turns. One would go off fishing while the
other stayed behind on the nest keeping
Little Albatross warm, keeping him safe.

Day by day, well fed, well guarded and
warm, Little Albatross grew ever bigger,
stronger, noisier, hungrier. Through the
softness of his down he was growing fine
white feathers. And now his wings were
long and wide and wonderful.

But not far away skulked a killer bird,
always watchful, always waiting, and
always still, so still they did not even
know he was there.

Then one bright day Mother and Father
Albatross looked at Little Albatross
and saw how big he was, and how strong.
It would be quite safe, they thought,
to leave him for a while and go off
fishing together.

So away they flew, out over the cliff top,
singing again their soaring song, the song
of the wandering albatross.

They did not see the killer bird beneath them. But the killer bird saw them.

He was watching. He was waiting.

"Oh Father! Oh Mother!" cried Little Albatross, who had never before been left on his own. "Come back! Come back!"

But the wind screamed and the waves roared, and they could not hear him.

Out over the surging sea they soared,
always on the look-out for silver flashing
fish swimming below them in the surging
sea. One glimpse was all they needed.

Down they dived, deep down into the
grey-green sea, hunting after fish.
Then up they came again, riding the
waves and swallowing all they had caught.

That night, Little Albatross slept alone
on his nest. He did not see the killer bird
skulking closer, closer.

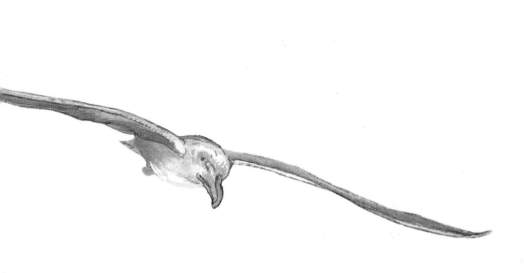

When morning came, Father and Mother
Albatross were still wandering the ocean
together, still soaring high above the
grey-green sea, when they saw a fishing
boat beneath them. And look! Following
behind were thousands upon thousands
of silver flashing fish. A feast of fish!

Down they dived at once, without ever
thinking, down into the surging sea,
where they snatched up fish after fish
after fish. Then up they swam, up
towards the light, up towards the air.

But they did not know that the fishing
nets were closing in around them.
They could not see them,
until they swam right into
them and were at once
caught up, held fast
and trapped.

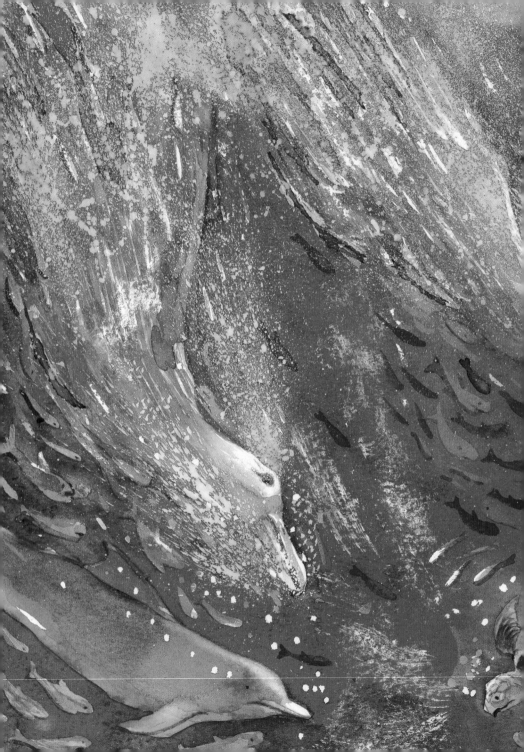

How they fought to free
themselves. How they
struggled.

But the more they fought
and struggled, the more
entangled they became.

They were helpless now
in the nets, and they were
not alone.

All around them they
saw not only thousands
of struggling fish, but
dolphins were caught up
too, and turtles as well.

Meanwhile . . .

Back on the cliff top, the killer bird skulked
ever closer. Closer.

And still Little Albatross had not seen him.

Father Albatross and Mother Albatross hung in the nets, still living, but only just. When they saw the grey shark-shadow coming up out of the depths of the ocean, they made one last bid to break free.

In his greed and in his rage, the shark attacked the nets, tearing them with terrible force.

But he was too late, for the fishermen were already winding in their nets. Up and out of the sea came the nets, filled with thousands upon thousands of fish.

And caught up in them were all the turtles and dolphins, and Mother Albatross and Father Albatross too.

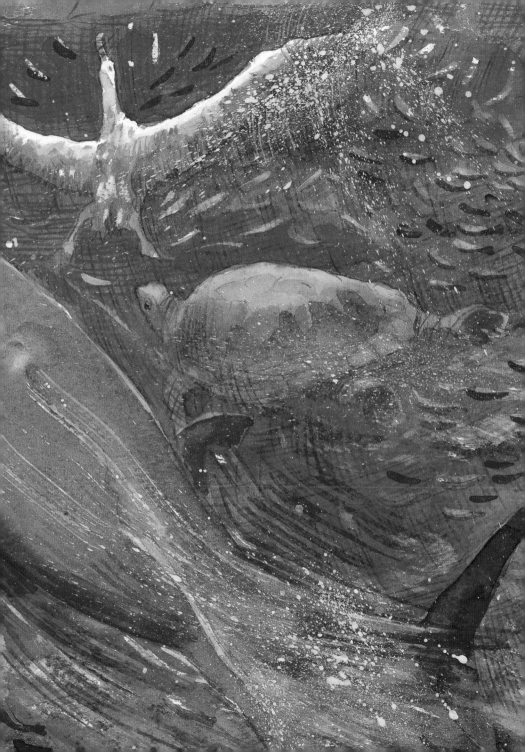

As soon as the fishermen saw
them, they freed them from
the nets. They could see
at once that the birds were
too tired to fly off. So the
fishermen let them rest.

They looked after them,
and fed them to make them
strong again. By the time
they flew off that evening,
the whole crew was there
to wave them off.

By now the killer bird was circling.
He was moving in for the kill.
He had waited long enough.

Little Albatross saw him coming,
and saw the killer glint in his eye.

"Oh Mother! Oh Father!" he cried.
"Help me! Help me!"

Suddenly, from high above them
came a chilling cry. Out of the sky
came Mother Albatross and Father
Albatross, like two great white arrows
aimed at the killer bird's heart.

He knew it would be death
to stay, and flew off at once.
Far out to sea they chased
him and harried him until
they were quite sure he
would never come back.

By the time they returned
Little Albatross was leaping
up and down, frantic to see
them, frantic for his food.
But he was cross too.

Oh Mother!" he cried.
en waiting for you for so long.
been so frightened, so hungry.
Where were you? What kept you?"

"It's a long story," said Father Albatross.

"We won't leave you again," said Mother
Albatross. "Promise."

"Feed me, Father! Feed me, Mother,"
cried Little Albatross.

"That's what we're here for," said
Mother Albtross. And they both fed
Little Albatross until he had eaten
himself happy.

Then he slept. And as he slept the first
snows of winter came falling all about
them. And the sound of their song
floated out over the grey-green sea,
the song of the wandering albatross.

About the Author

MICHAEL MORPURGO is one of Britain's best-loved writers for children and has won many prizes, including the Whitbread Prize, the Red House Children's Book Award and the Blue Peter Book Award. From 2003 to 2005 he was the Children's Laureate, a role which took him all over the UK to promote literacy and reading, and in 2005 he was named the Booksellers Association Author of the Year. In 2007 he was writer in residence at the Savoy Hotel in London. His bestselling novel *War Horse* has been turned into a hugely successful stage adaptation and film.

About the Illustrator

MICHAEL FOREMAN is one of the most talented and popular illustrators of children's books today. Twice winner of the Kate Greenaway Medal, his highly acclaimed books are published all over the world. He has illustrated over three hundred books, many of which he has written himself. He frequently collaborates with 'the other Michael'.

ALSO BY MICHAEL MORPURGO:

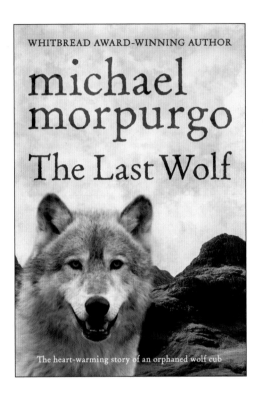

When Robbie McLeod finds an orphaned wolf
cub, Charlie, he vows to take care of him.
It is the beginning of an adventure that sweeps
boy and beast from the Highlands to the
high seas and beyond.

'Brings a slice of history to life'
TES

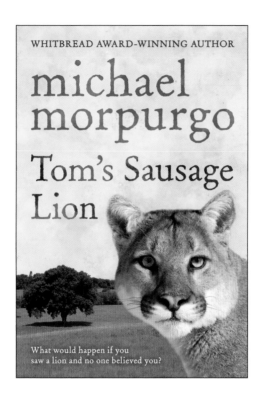

When Tom says he saw a lion strolling through the orchard with a string of sausages dangling from its mouth, no one believes him — except Clara, the cleverest girl in Tom's class. Clara knows something about Tom's story that no one else does — and together, they come up with a plan to prove Tom's telling the truth . . .

'Morpurgo writes with a fine mixture of clarity, depth and feeling' *Sunday Times*

~The~
Silver Swan

Michael Morpurgo
Illustrated by
Christian Birmingham

A thrilling and compassionate tale of a boy's
friendship with a swan, exquisitely complemented
by Christian Birmingham's dramatic,
luminous artwork.

'A truly wonderful book'
Guardian

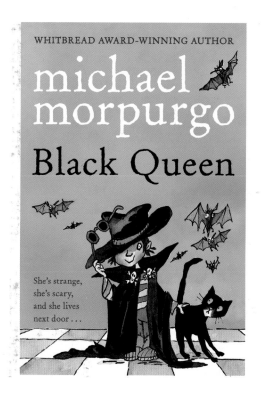

michael morpurgo

Black Queen

She's strange,
she's scary,
and she lives
next door . . .

The Black Queen is what Billy calls his spooky
next-door neighbour. She always wears a black cloak
and a wide-brimmed black hat, and lurks about
her garden with her black cat. When she's away,
Billy can't resist the opportunity to peek inside her
house, and sees chessboards scattered everywhere.
Who is the Black Queen, and what sort of game is
she playing? Billy thinks he knows . . .

'One of today's greatest storytellers'
The Bookseller